If Only...

A closed look came into his mother's eyes. 'What do you mean by that, Gordon?' she asked him.

'Well. I've been thinking that I want to know where Dad is— '

'*Where he is*?' she said. Her voice was strained now. 'But we *know* where he is, Gordon.'

'No. No we don't. That's just it!' Gordon banged the heel of his hand on his brow. 'Canada doesn't mean a thing, Mum. Canada's – *huge*. We don't have an *address*, do we? We don't know where he is exactly, do we?' His voice was squeaky with tension now.

'And I don't *want* to know! ' Mum said breathlessly. '*I don't want to know Gordon*,' she said insistently.

Gordon rushed upstairs, with one thought in his head. Nobody was going to put him off now. Come what may, he was going to find his father.

If Only...

Sue Vyner

Illustrated by
Robin Lawrie

Evans Brothers Limited

Published by Evans Brothers Limited
2A Portman Mansions
Chiltern Street
London W1U 6NR

First published 2001

British Library Cataloguing in Publication Data
Vyner, Sue
If Only
1. Children's Stories
I. Title
823.9'14 [J]

ISBN 0237523310

Series Editor: Julia Moffatt
Designer: Jane Hawkins
Printed in Malta by Gutenberg Press Limited

Chapter One

Gordon closed his maths homework and put it into his bag ready for the morning. Pleased with himself. He'd spent a long time over it to make sure it was right.

Gordon liked things to be right.

Hated things to be wrong. Like his name. Which he was stuck with.

How he hated his name.

He didn't know any other Gordons. There were none in his year at Ferguson's Secondary. As far as he could make out, none in the school.

Gordon. From the Greek word *Gordius.* Meaning Bold.

If only! *Old fashioned* more like it. That's what it was. And that's what people thought about *him*. Corny. Behind-The-Times. Out dated. Antiquated. Archaic. Obsolete. Old-fangled and Old-Hat. The list in the dictionary was endless.

He got onto his bed. Stretched and yawned. Then curled up tight.

He was stuck with *women* too.

His mother for a start. Who'd always treated him – still treated him – like he was a baby.

Then there was his sister, Amy. Sixteen going on sixty. More like another mother to him than a sister. Amy. From the Latin word meaning *Love*. Meaning the love of his mother's life. Born when they were a proper family. By the time he was born that was all over. Hence, *Gordon-the-bold*. Boldness being essential, he supposed, for someone born when their father had just left them. Not only left but gone to Canada. How much farther could he have gone, for heaven's sake?

Then there was Gran. Gran, who was always there for them. There for Mum when she was having a bad time. There for his sister when she was down. There to mother *him* when he needed it. Only he wasn't exactly short on the mothering front was he?

And *then* there'd been Miss Bernard, his first teacher at the village primary. Followed by Mrs Baker who was in charge till he left.

All these women in his life, and not one man! Even his grandfather had to go and die when Gordon was little. And Mum being an only child, there was no other family.

The thought that there might be family on his father's side always excited him. But not for long. Because if they were out there, they hadn't bothered to find *him*.

He smarted with a sense of injustice...

His friend Sean Taylor warned him: 'Boys like you grow up to be mummy's boys, Gord.' Making it sound really bad. The fact that Sean didn't have a father either, didn't apparently count. 'I've got nothing to worry about. My mum has so many boyfriends I'm glad of a bit of peace in-between times. But you, Gord!' he'd said, pursing his lips, 'you'll have to be very careful.'

Gordon threw himself round the bed, then settled on his back and stared up at the ceiling.

Ferguson's Secondary School had changed things, of course. Plenty of men about the place. But it was taking some getting used to. And that was the point. Gordon identified the shadows on the ceiling cast by the street light outside and remembered the time they'd frightened him too. But now they were just there weren't they? So perhaps that's how it would be at school eventually. Because if he admitted it, fear was a familiar feeling at Ferguson's Secondary. Fear of doing the wrong thing. Fear of anything he found difficult. Fear of bigger, older kids, and some teachers too.

He curled up on his side.

But he'd never be a mummy's boy he thought, because in this family it was more a case of mummy's girl. In this family his sister could do no wrong, while he could do no right. Because didn't *he* look like his father? And didn't his mum always say that as if it was the worst thing in life? Like he could help it. And like his father was some criminal. Which Gordon supposed he was, in a way. After all, he did leave them. Took off and went as far away as he could. And never heard of since. How many times had he heard his mum say what a criminal thing that was to do? Before adding, 'Good riddance to bad rubbish!'

So why complain about it so much, then? Gordon thought indignantly...

Sean Taylor was Gordon's only friend. They'd gone through the village primary together, then moved on to secondary school. Sean was someone to hang out with in the village. And someone to wander round the playground with at school. Sean wasn't afraid of anything or anybody.

Gordon closed his eyes and saw an image of himself.

Thirteen, going on fourteen. Tall for his age. But thin. With short dark hair that Mum still cut. It never used to bother him, but now made him feel self conscious.

Hairstyles were important at Ferguson's Secondary. At least Mum didn't run clippers over his head like Sean's mum, though. Because he had to agree with his mum that it made Sean look a bit of a thug. His hair wasn't as short as Sean's but he wished Mum would let him grow it longer. That would be cool. And it would set off his dark deep-set eyes and strong eyebrows to perfection. He wasn't so sure about the pale skin, though, it always made him look a bit sickly. And he wished he wasn't so thin. Tall. He liked that. But not thin.

As he drifted off into sleep Gordon projected this image into a man's body. It was the nearest he could get to an image of his father.

Chapter Two

At school, Gordon scrutinised Mr Benn, the new English teacher. Speciality, Drama.

Unlike Sean, Mr Benn's number two haircut didn't make him look like a thug. Instead, with his crinkle-eyes, dimple-in-chin, and trendy gear, it made him look really cool.

They hadn't done much Drama before Mr Benn. Just read through some boring old plays in class. But Mr Benn talked about it as if it was the most important thing in the curriculum.

All Gordon knew about Drama was what he'd done at the village primary. Where it had meant *listening* to *Peter and the Wolf* in year three, then *doing* it for a Parents' Assembly.

'Move like the wolf,' Miss Bernard had shouted.

'Make yourself into a tree.'

'Fly like a bird.'

'Feel the air round your wings!'

And they'd wafted their arms frantically up and down and raced round the room, dipping and diving and spinning like mad things. Later, at home he'd prowled round his bedroom – a wolf – a bird – a tree – Peter! And he'd loved the music ever since.

But *proper* Drama? Gordon thought that was what kids did on the telly. Like *Byker Grove*. *Grange Hill. Neighbours.*

Mr Benn had other ideas though.

Today, as they sat on the floor, he squatted down in the middle of them and pronounced, 'Drama is for everyone.' Then looked round at them.

A few kids sniggered. 'Huh! Prancing about, Sir, you mean,' Sean said. Probably remembering Miss Bernard too.

'Definitely no prancing about,' Mr Benn said, eyeing Sean and one or two others who looked like they wanted to disrupt the lesson. He stood up, looking at everyone and moving between them, then squatted down again.

The class regrouped round him.

'Drama allows the heart to fly. The body to escape,' he said. And the way he said it, nobody sniggered. 'It allows the mind to expand,' he continued. 'In fact, where some pupils are concerned—' he directed his stare at Sean and a few others '—drama is often the best way forward.'

It would have sounded high falluting coming from anyone else, but the way Mr Benn spoke made you want to believe him. Even Sean was quiet now.

'Drama,' Mr Benn continued. 'can help students avoid painful pitfalls. So.' He got up briskly, 'let's kick off today with—' he wrote on a board in huge letters '—RACE PREJUDICE IN SCHOOLS.'

The class eyed each other. Some pulled faces. A few giggled. A few looked embarrassed. Some looked angry and some just stared at the floor.

'Now. Think yourselves into a different skin,' Mr Benn continued. 'Black if you're white. White if you're black. Black if you're Asian. Mixed race. Get the idea?'

His eyes roamed restlessly round the class, drawing everyone in.

'Do you flaunt what you are?' he asked quietly. 'Or do you hide behind it? Do you feel threatened?'

Then he talked them through an imaginary situation in the playground.

Role play, he called it. And told them they'd be doing a lot of it in the future.

Whatever it was, as the lesson continued, everyone got caught up in what they were doing.

It felt weird putting yourself into somebody else's shoes. At first it worried Gordon. Then it fascinated him. And eventually he found himself saying and doing things that wouldn't have occurred to him before. By the time the lesson drew to a close, a new awareness told him that from now on, anyone stepping out of line in this direction would get it in the neck from him.

And from that day on, as far as Gordon was concerned, Drama was cool.

There was plenty more role play over the next few lessons. Bullying. Thieving. Drugs. Bunking off school. They experienced it all under Mr Benn's eagle-eyed supervision.

Then one day he wrote on the board in the by now familiar letters:

FAMILY RELATIONSHIPS

'Think yourself into a different situation,' Mr Benn said. 'Single parent family if you're in a two parent family. Single parent family being brought up by Dad if you're with Mum now. An only child if you're part of a big family. Part of a big family if you're an only one. The oldest if you're the youngest. The youngest if you're the oldest.' Then he'd posed the usual sort of questions. 'How does this change things? Does it change the way you're treated? Does it change the way you think about yourself? The way others see you?'

Gordon could identify with the roles on several fronts. For example, he'd often wished he was the oldest in the family – then there'd be no more babying, and Mum would depend on him instead of on Amy. And when it came to the discussion part of the exercise he surprised himself by saying so.

Mr Benn was circulating and dropping in on the discussions. 'That's a good point Gordon,' he said.

But Gordon didn't find it so easy when it came to pretending to be in a two parent family. In fact he couldn't handle this, and got very uptight. Mr Benn spotted his difficulty straight away though. 'You can only take role play so far,' he said quietly to Gordon, then nodded his head at him as if to say he was doing fine. He advised the group to move onto another scenario.

Gordon was grateful. Mr Benn was definitely the best teacher ever, he decided.

It was later in the term that Mr Benn told them about the play he'd written. And that the school was going to perform the play at the end of term.

'Forget Shakespeare for now,' he said triumphantly. 'Think *Benn*! You heard it here first. You saw it here first. Or you will. At the end of term.'

Sean stifled a yawn.

'Am I boring you, Sean?' Mr Benn said.

Sean shook his head. 'No, Sir. Sorry, Sir. I had a heavy night last night, though.' The boy sitting next to him knocked Sean's elbow and Sean collapsed with a groan.

'*You* had a heavy night, Sean?' Mr Benn said. 'You don't know you're born. Me? I had marking. Preparation. The muse!' He swept the back of his hand over his forehead in dramatic mode, and everyone laughed. 'You have no idea, Sean.'

Mr Benn grinned at Sean, then looked round the class.

'But back to my play,' he said. 'Title. *The Perfect Imperfect.*'

Curious faces stared at each other.

'A title to intrigue, eh?' Mr Benn studied their faces. 'But don't look so worried. It only reflects what's happening right now in your lives and mine. And covers some of the issues we've been acting out in class.' When he paused, Gordon concentrated hard. Because Mr Benn's pauses usually meant there was something coming up that merited thinking about. 'I've seen a lot of promise in this class,' he finally said. 'So I hope several of you will come along to audition for my play at lunch time today.'

'I suppose all the best parts will go to the older kids,' Chloe Watson said.

'Not at all, Chloe,' Mr Benn said. 'There's a range of parts for all ages. And they'll be cast purely on ability.'

'You can't refuse me then, Sir, can you?' Hayley Bishop said with a wicked grin.

'Come along and find out, Hayley,' Mr Benn said.

On the way out of the lesson, Gordon heard Mr Benn sigh heavily. He turned round. 'When I do that, Sir, my mum says it can't be as bad as all that,' he said.

'And your mum's right,' Mr Benn said. 'But I've put a lot of work into this play Gordon. Burned the midnight oil,' he continued. 'And now it's over to someone else to make something of it.' He frowned. 'What will you make of it, I wonder, Gordon?'

'Me, sir?' How come it was suddenly up to him? Gordon felt flustered.

'Not you, personally, Gordon. But you – like in representing all the students. I've got to trust my play to you lot!' He sighed again. 'And who will turn up at lunch time, I wonder?' he said, chewing on his bottom lip.

'I'll come if you like, Sir,' Gordon found himself saying. Just to please Mr Benn, who beamed. 'That's my boy, Gordon!'

When he arrived for the auditions, Gordon wondered
what he'd let himself in for. It was one thing to do
role play in class. But here, on your own, exposed, in
front of kids *and* teachers? That was something else.

He watched the banter between groups of boys and
girls, old and young, and envied them. He wondered if
it would ever be that easy for him.

Mr Benn was there, and Miss Wright – another
English teacher – and Miss More – PE and Dance.

Each of them looking round to see who was turning up.

Gordon didn't think he stood much chance of a part, thank goodness. He'd only come because he felt sorry for Mr Benn, hadn't he?

Miss More put some music on, then asked them to interpret it in any way they thought. Back to *Peter and the Wolf*! Gordon thought. Perhaps Miss Bernard had been on the right track after all – except that this music was pop music, and kids were straight into the

slinky, sexy movements he felt ridiculous even attempting.

'It's only a warmer. You don't have to join in if you don't want to,' Mr Benn said. 'If this isn't for you, just watch.'

Gordon relaxed.

When the music stopped, Miss More selected a group of dancers and took them off somewhere.

'And now, for those who want to audition for the speaking parts, it's your turn,' Mr Benn said.

There was a nervous twittering as he sorted them into groups and handed round sheets of paper. Gordon nearly lost his nerve and made his escape. But Mr Benn pushed a sheet into his hand.

As he read it, Gordon was immediately intrigued. It was about fourteen year old Brad. What a great name! But Brad was in trouble with everyone. Family, school, and the police. And in the extract Gordon had to read, Brad was trying to convince his parents he was going to change.

Several boys read for the part before Gordon. And when it was his turn, though he was plagued by nerves, he focussed on the words and gave it his best. As he always did.

When it was over, Mr Benn nodded. 'I'll let you know,' he said.

When Mr Benn approached him, Gordon was stunned.

'I liked the way you read the part, Gordon,' Mr Benn said. 'You had a real feeling for it. As if you understood it. Would you like to be Brad?'

Chapter Three

Gordon had always been *slow at coming forward*, as his mother put it. In fact, he never shone at anything. So today, he couldn't wait to get home and tell her and Amy that Mr Benn had chosen *him* to play the main character in his play.

He wanted to wait till Mum was home, and tell them together. So when he got home, he dashed upstairs to read the play through.

And as he read, he lost all sense of time. When he was finished, he lay back on the bed and clasped his hands behind his head, then let out a long breath. 'Phew!' he hissed.

The Perfect Imperfect, was about a family. Dad, a successful business man. Mum who worked in a bank. And two kids. A model daughter, Stephanie, 11. And Brad, 14.

The perfect family.

Supposedly.

Except that Brad was the son from hell. A tearaway who showed no respect to his parents. Got expelled from school. Smoked, and experimented with drugs. And hung around clubs with delinquents. Including girls.

So.

Anything *but* the perfect family.

In the play, the only thing that got Brad back on the straight and narrow was a friend who wouldn't give up on him when his family had.

It started Gordon off thinking about his own family. He reflected that other one parent families got on fine. It seemed to make no difference to them that one parent was missing. But it had *always* made a difference to his family, he thought. Though he'd never ever seen his father, it was like he haunted them. And this despite the fact that his mother would never have a proper conversation about him. The only time she mentioned his dad was in passing, and always in a negative way.

So surely, his family had to be as far from perfect as it was possible to get?

But then he thought about the play. And Brad's family. And it got him thinking differently. Even when everything was supposedly perfect – things could still go badly wrong...

So. Was there any such thing as the perfect family, he asked himself?

And wondered, was that the point?

Suddenly Gordon wasn't sure he could do this. He couldn't be less like Brad if he tried, so how could he become him, even for a few hours?

Then he remembered how he'd felt when he read the part. Just like he *was* Brad. Capable of, and able to do all the things Brad did.

And Mr Benn said he'd read the part convincingly. *He* obviously thought he could do it...

He heard his mother come in and rushed down to tell them the news.

Amy was watching *Neighbours*, but at the mention of Mr Benn, pricked up her ears. No doubt something to do with the crinkle eyes and dimple-in-chin. 'I can't believe you went to the auditions. I didn't know you had it in you. I didn't know you were into that sort of thing,' she said, shocked.

It was a typical Amy reaction. Thought he had no initiative.

'Acting?' was all his mother said.

Another typical reaction. Probably thought it wasn't worth doing.

Gordon was furious.

'Mr Benn says Drama improves social skills,' he said, desperately trying to impress them. But coming from him it definitely sounded high falluting.

'Social skills? his mum repeated doubtfully. 'But what you need today is qualifications, Gordon. That's the only thing will get you a good job.'

Gordon tried again. 'But Mr Benn says Drama builds confidence. He says it teaches a better understanding of emotions... ' His voice trailed off and he felt deflated. 'If Amy had been chosen, you'd have been dead pleased for her,' he said, glaring at Mum.

'Of course I'm pleased for you,' Mum said quickly. 'If you're pleased, I am. You know that. But I am your mother, aren't I? And I only want what's best for you. There's no one else to look out for you, is there?'

She couldn't resist the dig. And then gave one of her long, wounded sighs.

Gordon got up. 'I'm going upstairs,' he said...

It wasn't difficult getting into the role. It wasn't difficult learning the lines. Not at home. In his room. Practising on his own.

But rehearsals were something else. In front of all those people.

They were all in the same boat though, weren't they?

And soon, not being himself was – well – wicked.

As Brad, Gordon got to do and say things that wouldn't normally enter his obedient little head. Like cheeking adults. Bunking off school. Thieving. Smoking. And even kissing a girl – this was the hardest thing he had to do – though definitely the best! Even Sean was impressed.

As Brad, everything seemed to click into place. As if he was actually a different person. And being called Brad was, well, *cool*.

So if he *had* been called Brad then – would it have made him a different person? It was a question he thought about a lot while they rehearsed. And one he couldn't answer. One of *life's little mysteries* he thought to himself – which was one of Gran's favourite sayings.

As rehearsals progressed, Gordon got to know Brad as well as if he was a real person. And he began to see Brad in characters around school. In lots of ways he envied him. Then again, he was usually relieved to slip back into his own shoes. All that wickedness was great fun. But exhausting. Gordon didn't think he'd have the stamina in real life.

On the night of the first performance, Mum and Amy came with Mum's friend, Ellie Wilkinson. Ellie and Mum both worked as receptionists at a dental practice in town.

Hayley Bishop, who played one of Gordon's girl friends, nearly went into a swoon when she forgot her words. And when Gordon prompted her she flashed him a grateful smile. Then someone nearly tripped over a wire on the floor, but managed to recover in time to camouflage the mistake. But apart from that, the play went brilliantly.

And at the end, the applause was amazing. It gave Gordon a buzz like nothing else he'd experienced before.

When he got home Mum's friend was there too. She sprang up and hugged him. 'You were brilliant, Gordon. Brilliant!'

His mum smiled warmly. 'You were, Gordon. Really good. You stole the show!' She sounded and looked proud and gave him a hug too.

Amy put her thumbs up. 'Well done little bruv,' she said.

The triumph! Gordon was weak with relief and a lump came to his throat. He swallowed hard. 'It was just acting,' he said and shrugged his shoulders casually.

Ellie rolled her eyes. 'God, Maggie, it'd be a nightmare to have a kid like that Brad,' she said.

Mum's eyes widened too. 'You're not joking,' she said.

'We're lucky with our kids, aren't we?' Ellie said.

Mum nodded her head, 'Very lucky,' she said, and beamed at Gordon.

In bed that night, Gordon thought about Brad.

Had Mr Benn known someone like him? he wondered. Had there been a Brad in Mr Benn's family? He felt sorry for him if there had. But then, perhaps that's what made Mr Benn such a good teacher...

Chapter Four

After the last performance, the headmaster got up onto the stage. First he congratulated the cast on a *splendid* performance, then called for Mr Benn to come on stage too. 'It's not every school can boast their own playwright,' he said proudly.

Everybody stamped and cheered him, and Mr Benn did an exaggerated bow, then said he couldn't have done it without his *magnificent* cast. When the cast took another bow, Mr Benn singled Gordon out and drew him forward. The audience stood up and cheered.

After the play, Gordon was a bit of a celebrity round the school.

Kids would call after him, 'What mischief have you been up to today then, Brad?' and he would make an appropriate retort.

Gordon was suddenly Mr Cool. And he loved it.

So what was in a name after all, then? And did it really matter?

Well. It was as Brad, not Gordon, that he was Mr Cool.

Gordon wished his name was Brad.

Suddenly it was the end of term. And when he broke up, to his surprise, Gordon found himself missing school.

Mum always got stressed out at Christmas. But this year it was worse than ever. The nearer Christmas got, the worse things got. She said the shops were too hot. Too crowded. The queues too long. There was too much to do.

With two days to go before the big day, she dragged herself and Amy round the supermarket for a final time. And when they got home she collapsed into a chair.

It was then Gordon noticed how terrible she looked.

Amy went into the kitchen to put the shopping away and make her a cup of tea.

Gordon followed. 'What's the matter with Mum?' he asked.

Amy looked exasperated. 'For heaven's sake!' she said. 'Haven't you noticed how much extra work there is for her at Christmas? She's exhausted.'

'Oh. Is that all?' he said.

He thought Amy was going to hit him.

'I only said that because I was worried it was something bad,' he said quickly. 'I thought she was poorly.'

The next day it was something bad. One minute she was hot with a fever, then she was shaking and shivering with cold. By mid afternoon her breathing was laboured. And with Gran away for Christmas, Amy panicked.

'Let's call an ambulance,' Gordon said, expecting Amy to say there was no need for that. So that when she did, he knew how serious it was. He panicked too.

And when the ambulance men carried Mum into the ambulance and drove off, Gordon was beside himself with worry.

And it was Christmas!

The next thing Gordon knew, Amy was packing his bag.

'Mum said you're to go to the Wilkinsons for a few days,' she announced.

Gordon was gobsmacked. He wasn't a baby to be bundled up and sent away. 'Why can't I stay here with you?' he said.

'Because I'm going to stay with Emma,' Amy said. Emma was Amy's best friend.

Gordon flounced round the room.

Tomorrow he wanted to get up early like he always did. He wanted his stocking and his stocking presents. And later, he wanted to get up and open the rest of his presents with Amy and Mum. And at lunch time he wanted to eat the best dinner ever. Mum always said there was no one, anywhere, sat down to a better Christmas dinner.

Christmas with strangers wasn't on.

He stomped round his room in a fury. It wasn't fair.

Chapter Five

When Mr Wilkinson arrived to pick him up, he rested an arm on Gordon's shoulder. 'Bad luck old man,' he said. 'We Wilkinsons will do our best for you, though.'

He was a big man with a gruff voice and a lot of hair on his face as well as his head. Gordon was tall for his age, but Mr Wilkinson dwarfed him.

He must have noticed the worry on Gordon's face because he said, 'Your mother's in the best place, Gordon. They'll soon get her better. In the meantime, we'll look after you. No need to worry about a thing...'

When they went into the Wilkinson's kitchen, Mrs Wilkinson was stuffing the biggest turkey Gordon had ever seen. When she saw Gordon she spread buttery palms out to him and smiled.

Mr Wilkinsons eyes lit up. 'Do you need any help with that brute?' he asked.

Mrs Wilkinson shook her head. 'Not for the minute,' she said.

'I've never seen one as big as that!' Gordon exclaimed.

Wilkinson rubbed his large belly. 'Well this takes some filling up,' he said, his eyes laughing.

'Daddy always says he gets a turkey big enough to feed an army,' a little boy said. 'It's a family trad – trad—'

'Tradition,' his father said. 'This is George, Gordon. He's six.'

'And I'm Becky,' a little girl said.

'And she's only three,' George said.

'But I'm nearly as big as him!' Becky said indignantly.

'Call me Ellie, and Mr Wilkinson Eddie,' Mrs Wilkinson said to Gordon. She finished with the turkey and washed her hands. Then she looked at her family. 'I saw Gordon in his school play,' she told them. 'He had the main part, and he was very, very, good.'

Becky pouted. 'I was Mary in the 'Tivity at nursewy, Mummy,' she reminded her mother. 'I born baby Jesus in the cow shed. And I was vewy vewy good.'

George tutted. 'That's not acting, Becky,' he said. 'That's just nursery stuff.'

Becky's lip dropped.

'Of course you were Mary, and you were very very good,' Ellie said with a big smile. Then she changed the subject. 'Can you take Gordon upstairs, George, and show him where he's sleeping?'

At the top of the stairs, George stopped and turned round. 'You're sharing my room,' he said with a heavy frown. 'I've never shared my room with a *strange* boy before. Only with my cousin, Peter.'

Gordon didn't like the idea either. But he'd been so busy feeling sorry for himself, it hadn't occurred to him he might be spoiling things for anyone else.

They went into George's bedroom.

'I'm the top bunk,' George said anxiously.

Gordon couldn't care less which bunk he was in. He just wished everything was normal and he could go home...

When they went back downstairs, Gordon wondered self-consciously what to do next.

Ellie came in and sat down on the sofa. She patted the empty place next to her, but Becky pounced into it. Ellie grabbed Becky and sat her on her knee. Gordon sat down stiffly.

'Pass the bowl, Eddie,' Ellie said to Mr Wilkinson,
who passed over a bowl full of sweets and nuts. 'We
like to sample things on Christmas Eve, Gordon.
Seeing as we don't have any room for extras over the
next few days.'

'Oh yes we do,' Becky yelled.

'Oh no we don't,' Mr Wilkinson boomed.

'Oh yes we do!' Becky and George yelled together.

Becky grabbed a handful of sweets and shoved them
into her mouth. 'These are my favouwites, Gordun,'
she spluttered.

'Gordon can see they are Becky. But you don't need to shovel them all in at once,' her mother said.

Gordon helped himself to some. Then some more. Things were looking up.

'Will you get the Littlies washed now, Eddie, and into their jim-jams?' Ellie said.

Becky bounced off her mum's knee and stamped her feet. 'It's Cwistmas Eve,' she wailed.

'But if you don't get to bed and off to sleep good and early tonight, you'll delay Father Christmas, won't you?' Mr Wilkinson said, bright eyed. He shook his head and sucked in his breath. 'Father Christmas has got a heavy night ahead of him, Becky, and he relies on children like you to be good, so he can get on with his deliveries!'

Becky's shoulders hunched and she giggled. 'All wight, Daddy,' she said.

Mr Wilkinson heaved himself out of his chair and scooped the kids up, one in each arm. Ellie disappeared into the kitchen. Mr Wilkinson nodded at Gordon. 'When these urchins are in bed, Ellie and me have got things to do,' he said. 'But the TV zapper's there, and help yourself to the goodies.' Then he disappeared upstairs.

Gordon zapped through all the TV stations several times for the fun of it, then settled for a film which Mum probably wouldn't let him watch. Then he tucked into the goodies. Things were definitely looking up.

Later, he heard Ellie and Eddie moving about in the kitchen and went to see what they were doing. Eddie was peeling potatoes while Ellie was doing something with the other vegetables.

They smiled when they saw him. 'The trick is to get as much done as possible tonight, Gordon,' Ellie said. 'I suppose your mum does the same.'

Gordon's brow puckered. Yes. She did. But it wasn't a team effort like it was here.

He frowned. Realising for the first time just how hard that was on her...

He woke up abruptly and wondered what had woken him and where he was.

Someone shone a torch on him, then started scrabbling about.

'Wake up Gordon,' George hissed.

'I'm awake,' Gordon said.

George scrambled down the ladder and put the main light on.

Gordon blinked.

'We open our big presents downstairs. But I always have some presents in my stocking,' George hissed. 'Have you got a stocking, Gordon?'

Gordon was ridiculously relieved to see his old much used stocking at the foot of the bed. He reached down it and pulled out the computer game he'd asked for, and a CD. And then he found a small box full of pink gooey stuff and giggled. Ever since Sean had brought one to school after the Christmas holidays last year he'd wanted one of these. He dug his fingers into the gunge in the box and squeezed. It made a very rude noise.

George warned Gordon they'd get murdered if they woke the others up, so they giggled as quietly as they could.

And eventually dozed off again.

Till somebody bounced on Gordon. 'Wake up. He's *been*!' Becky yelled.

It was seven o'clock.

Eddie appeared in the doorway and scratched his belly, which was hanging over his pyjama trousers. 'Let Gordon wake up before you bounce on him, Becky,' he said.

Too late.

Gordon groaned.

'Did you sleep all right, son?' Eddie asked.

'Yes thank you, Eddie,' Gordon said.

Eddie reached up and grabbed George out of bed. Gave him a bear-hug. 'Happy Christmas, George,' he said.

George put both arms round his dad's neck and hugged him back. 'Happy Christmas, Daddy.'

'I see you boys have been awake already,' Eddie said. 'So what have you both got, then?'

When Gordon got his box of goo and squeezed it, Eddie laughed so much his belly wobbled.

Then Becky grabbed Eddie by both hands. 'Come and see my pwesents, Daddy,' she said.

Ellie appeared in the doorway, rubbing her eyes. 'What on earth's all the fuss about?' she said in a pretend cross voice. 'Is there something happening today?'

'You know, Mummy,' Becky screamed. 'It's Cwistmas!'

'Oh, I forgot,' Ellie said and Becky screamed louder.

'Oh no you didn't, Mummy!'

Gordon squeezed the gunge and it produced a loud fart.

Ellie doubled up with laughter.

Usually, Christmas Day was a bit of an anti climax after the presents were opened – what to do till dinner time – but today wasn't like that. Because Eddie appeared with an armful of coats. 'Coats on,' he demanded. 'A breath of fresh air in the park to work up the appetite – and to give the skateboards a workout, eh kids?'

'Don't want to go out,' Becky said, and stamped her feet. 'Want to play with my Barbie make-up.'

'She's always a pain. Never wants to leave her presents, Gordon,' George said confidentially. 'I didn't used to, either. But now I'm older, I quite like to go out for a bit.'

Eddie grinned and Gordon giggled. Sharing the joke. He felt like one of the grown ups.

When they got back, the house smelt delicious. And Gordon was suddenly homesick.

'Do you want to give the hospital a ring?' Ellie said. 'I rang while you were out and your mum's comfortable. But she wanted to speak to you.'

When he rang, Mum said she was feeling much better. 'Happy Christmas, Gordon,' she said.

'Happy Christmas,' Gordon replied. A lump in his throat.

Then he rang Amy.

Eddie set the table. That done, he opened a bottle of wine. He poured a glass for himself and Ellie, then poured a smaller glass and gave it to Gordon. 'It's Christmas,' he said with a wink.

Gordon took it and grinned.

Becky pouted. 'I want some wine,' she said.

Eddie made a big fuss of clinking some ice into two tall glasses and dropping slices of lemon into the coke before adding corkscrew straws. And when he handed the drinks to George and Becky they squealed excitedly.

It seemed like everything Eddie did, he had the knack of making it special.

'Raise your glasses, then,' he said. 'Cheers, me dears, and Happy Christmas everybody,' he boomed in a voice which could have belonged to Father Christmas himself.

'Happy Christmas!' they all yelled.

Eddie kissed the end of Ellie's nose.

Gordon looked embarrassed, but the Littlies just giggled.

When Eddie walked in carrying the turkey they all cheered. Then Eddie made another big fuss over the carving – like it was the most important thing he'd ever done. Cutting each piece and arranging it carefully on the plate then licking his lips.

Gordon watched, wide eyed.

When they all had their food, Ellie let out a big breath then tucked into her meal heartily.

It had been another real team effort. And once again, it occurred to Gordon how different it was for Mum.

'It's lovely, Ellie,' he said shyly.

Ellie beamed. 'That's all right then, isn't it?'

So it all ended up A-OK. And spending these few days with the Wilkinsons helped Gordon understand a few things.

Like – it was better, and easier, with two parents around.

Like – if Mum had someone like Eddie in her life, things would be very different.

So why there were so many one parent families around then, he wondered?

For another thing, it was good to experience first hand what it was like not being the youngest in the household. At the Wilkinsons no one, but no one, babied him. And it meant a lot more to him than a glass of wine. Although being expected to do more to help was sometimes a bit of a bore.

Gordon made up his mind that when he went home, things were going to be very different.

When Mum came out of hospital and he went home, he told her how he felt.

'I'm thirteen,' he said, 'and sometimes you treat me

like I'm three!'

As she lay on the sofa, Mum just smiled indulgently at him. 'But you are my baby,' she said matter-of-factly, and ruffled his hair.

It was the worst thing she could have said or done.

Gordon shrugged her off. 'It was great being the oldest at Eddie's and Ellie's, Mum,' he said indignantly. 'They didn't baby me. And they depended on me to help with the Littlies. You never depend on me. It's not fair, Mum.'

Mum looked at Gordon thoughtfully. Then she said, 'You're right!' – as if she'd only just realised it – 'You're absolutely right!' she repeated, and went a bit red in the face. 'It's going to be hard not to think of you as the baby of the family, Gordon, but I'll try to stop it. I promise I'll try.'

Gordon grinned.

Chapter Six

Before he knew it he was back at school. And a bit disappointed when people forgot about Brad.

He missed Brad. And decided that when he grew up he was going to be an actor. One day he'd be well known. Live in London. Travel the world.

Go to Canada...

One Friday evening the phone rang.

'It's Eddie,' Mum said. 'And he wants to talk to you, Gordon.' She handed the phone to Gordon.

'I've got tickets to the rugby match tomorrow,' Eddie said. 'Nobody's interested in coming at this end. I wondered if you'd like to come with me, Gordon?'

'Cool!' Gordon said down the phone. It wasn't just the rugby. It would be nice to see Eddie again. 'See you tomorrow then,' he said excitedly.

'Wicked!' he said to Mum. 'I've never been to a live match before.'

It was wildly exciting at the match, and Eddie shouted himself silly. Gordon did his best to keep up with him.

By half time they were both hoarse. Eddie gave Gordon a throat pastille to suck. 'I always have them in my pocket on a match day,' he said with a laugh.

Gordon looked round at the crowd, then back at Eddie. 'I wish my dad was here with me,' he suddenly said.

It was the first time he'd mentioned his dad to Eddie.

Eddie rested his arm loosely on Gordon's shoulder. 'I wish he was too, Gordon,' he said. Then he tightened the grip on Gordon's shoulder. 'But in the meantime, any time you want to come with me, just give us a shout.'

Gordon grinned gratefully. 'I'll take you up on that,' he said.

Gordon arrived home hoarse and freezing cold, but glowing with excitement.

And he couldn't stop talking.

Mum went a bit quiet. 'I didn't know you liked rugby that much,' she said.

'I didn't know either. But now I do, Eddie says he'll take me any time,' he said.

Another day, Mum came home from work and told him the Wilkinsons were going away in their caravan for half term. 'Ellie says there's room for you, so would you like to go with them? I said it was nice of them to ask, but you probably wouldn't. The kids being so young and everything. Not much company for you.'

But she was wrong. 'Yes!' Gordon said eagerly. 'I'd love to go. It'll be great.'

Mum went quiet again. 'All these places you're going. Without us,' she said.

Gordon frowned. 'But we don't go to places like Eddie and Ellie,' he said.

Mum frowned.

'You don't mind me going do you, Mum?' he said. Gordon couldn't think of one good reason why Mum should mind him going away with the Wilkinsons.

Mum shrugged. 'Course I don't mind. I just wish—'
She didn't finish the sentence.

Was she wishing they were a family like the Wilkinsons? he wondered. And suddenly felt sorry for her. He went and put his arm round her. 'I won't go,' he said.

She grabbed his arm. 'Of course you must go, love,' she said earnestly. 'Take no notice of me – I just wish I could do all the things with you that you want to do.'

As half term approached, Gordon watched the weather forecast carefully. He wanted the weather to hold because Eddie had told him that if it did, they'd go walking and rock climbing and things like that. 'And we'll hire a boat out. Go fishing,' he'd said.

Rugby. Now fishing. Things were on the up again.

The morning they were going away, Gordon leapt out of bed and pulled the curtains back.

Sunlight streamed through the window. The sky was a steely blue.

'Yesss!' Gordon said and punched the air.

He dragged on his clothes. Ran downstairs.

Mum was eating toast, reading the paper. Amy still in bed.

Mum put the paper down. 'It's going to be strange without you around the place,' she said.

Gordon went up to her and planted a kiss on her cheek.

She put her hand up and touched the spot with the back of her hand. 'Don't be in too much of a hurry to grow up, Gordon,' she said softly.

Gordon frowned. Once the baby of the family, always the baby, he thought with a sigh...

When Gordon saw the people carrier towing the caravan, his eyes opened wide. 'Wow!' he exclaimed.

'Good eh? Hop in,' Eddie said.

Gordon got in.

Becky leaned across and put her hand on his arm. 'Hello, Gordun. Are you coming with us then?' she asked solemnly.

'Course he's coming, Stupid. Why do you think he's getting in the car if he's not coming with us?' George said.

'I'm not stupid. George says I'm stupid, Mummy,' Becky wailed.

'Nobody's stupid. And Gordon *is* coming with us,' Ellie said soothingly.

'Good!' Becky put her hand in Gordon's.

George turned up his nose. 'Yuk!' he said.

Gordon waved to Mum...

During the journey the Littlies didn't stop quarrelling. So when they arrived at the caravan site, Ellie let them out with a huge sigh of relief. They dashed over to some rocks and started climbing as if they'd been caged for hours.

'They always make a bee line for those rocks,' Ellie said. 'They love this site.'

Eddie positioned the caravan into place, and Gordon helped him unhitch it.

'I hope my two are as helpful as you when they're your age,' Eddie said.

Not for the first time, Gordon found himself wishing that Eddie was his dad...

While he was with them, he had the same thought over and over.

Which led him to think more and more about his own dad.

Because, after all, he *did* actually *have* a dad.

Somewhere out there...

'I wish my dad was like you,' he said to Eddie one morning as they scrambled over some rocks. 'He wouldn't have left us then.'

Eddie stopped and helped George up onto a rock with him. Then they sat on the rock and looked at the view.

'It's hard to understand what happens when people split up,' Eddie said, looking into the distance. 'And it's specially hard on the kids.' He looked at Gordon now. 'It's rotten for any kid to grow up not knowing their dad,' he said solemnly.

Nobody had ever said that to him before. But once said, it was so obvious that Gordon's heart lurched.

George called from lower down and they scrambled down to rejoin the others.

Eddie picked up George, put him on his shoulder, and they walked on.

As they walked, Gordon thought about what Eddie had said.

Why couldn't Mum have married somebody like Eddie instead of someone like his dad? he found himself asking.

Except that he didn't actually know what his dad was like, *did* he?

It's rotten for any kid to grow up not knowing their dad, Eddie had said.

Which got Gordon thinking...

'It was excellent, Mum,' he said for the nth time on getting home. 'One day we hired a boat and all of us went on the lake and I rowed with Eddie. The next day, the Littlies wanted to go to the camp park, so Ellie took them and Eddie and me went out in a boat on our own. Fishing. Eddie showed me how and I helped him catch a big one.' He held his hands wide. 'It was a whopper,' he said. 'Then the next day we went walking over the moors. Eddie gave George a piggyback and I gave Becky a piggyback and I wasn't tired. And the next day we went to this rocky place. It was magic. Like walking on the moon. And I helped Eddie with the Littlies because they were a bit scared and Ellie was too because it was a bit slippery. And the rest of the time we played round the camp site. There were these brilliant rocks to climb and a stream and we found a newt. And at night in the caravan we played games. Ellie's very good at games. She always wins.' He paused for breath.

Mum's eyebrows were raised. 'Well!' she said. 'You certainly found your get-up-and-go didn't you? You usually mope around on holiday.'

Then she picked up the paper and started reading it.

Gordon was hurt. It was as if she didn't want to know about the holiday.

'That's not true,' he said.

When she looked up from the paper he started again. 'It's just we don't do things like that on holiday,' he said. 'It's different with Ellie and Eddie.'

'It certainly is,' Mum said, then she put her paper down and stared at Gordon. 'It *is* different with them. It's bound to be. With us – well it's just us. You and me and Amy. Not so much fun...' She let out one of her sighs.

For once it didn't put Gordon off. 'Well. Being with them. It's made me think—' he said.

His mother looked at him expectantly.

'—Well – it's made me think about my dad...' Gordon said anxiously.

A closed look came into his mother's eyes. 'What do you mean by that, Gordon?' she asked him.

'Well. I've been thinking that I want to know where he is— '

'*Where he is?*' she said. Her voice was strained now. 'But we *know* where he is, Gordon.'

'No. No we don't. That's just it!' Gordon banged the heel of his hand on his brow. 'Canada doesn't mean a thing, Mum. Canada's – *huge*. We don't have an *address*, do we? We don't know where he is exactly, do we?' His voice was squeaky with tension now.

'And I don't *want* to know! ' Mum said breathlessly. '*I don't want to know Gordon*,' she said insistently.

Gordon rushed upstairs, with one thought in his head. Nobody was going to put him off now. Come what may, he was going to find his father.

Chapter Seven

But how?

At first he thought about asking Eddie for help. But Ellie being Mum's friend made that impossible. Ellie wouldn't do anything to upset Mum, would she? And Eddie wouldn't do anything to upset Ellie.

Then there was Gran. But she wouldn't do anything to upset Mum either.

So who else was there?

Then he thought about Mr Benn...

He remembered how sympathetic Mr Benn had been when they'd done all that about *family relationships* – how he'd seemed to understand how he felt. Perhaps Mr Benn would know what he should do now?

The next day, at dinner time, Gordon went to find Mr Benn.

Gordon breathed heavily. Nobody had ever said that to him before.

It reminded him of what Eddie had said about it being rotten for a child growing up not knowing his father – once said, so obvious that it had made his heart lurch. His heart lurched again now.

'*Good riddance to bad rubbish* – that's all my mum ever says about my dad,' he said.

'Tell me exactly what you do know about him, then, Gordon,' Mr Benn said.

'Nothing, Sir. Mum never talks about him properly. She sighs a lot, though.'

'Ahhh! Mothers often have a lot to sigh about though, don't they?' Mr Benn said.

'Especially if they're on their own, Sir.'

'Yes. Point taken, Gordon. So when did you – when did anyone – last hear from this father of yours? And where was he then?'

'I only know he's in Canada. And as far as I know no one's heard from him, Sir.'

'Right.' Mr Benn was biting his bottom lip. 'Right. That is a problem.'

'But you're good at problems, Sir,' Gordon said confidently. 'You said all that role-play is about problem-solving, didn't you?' Gordon was confident that Mr Benn would come up with something.

Mr Benn nodded his head. 'Uncles, aunts, grandparents, on his side?' he asked.

Gordon spread his hands. 'Don't know.'

'Friends?'

Gordon shrugged.

'*No one?*'

'I know he married again, Sir.' His shoulders slumped.

Mr Benn leaned over the table. 'But you're still his son, Gordon. And he's still your father. Always will be. Don't forget that.'

Gordon wanted this to be a comfort, but somehow it wasn't.

'What about your sister?' Mr Benn said. 'How old was she when your father left?'

'She was three when I was born, Sir. And that's when he went.'

'So she'll possibly remember him.' He paused. 'It must have been very hard on her.' He sighed. 'What does Amy have to say about it all, then?'

'She thinks the same as Mum. *Good riddance to bad rubbish.* She clams up at the mention of his name.'

Mr Benn stood up. Stuffed a file into his bag. 'Let's leave it for now, Gordon. Give me time to talk to a few people. See what I can come up with.'

'No! No, Sir!' Gordon said, panicking. 'You mustn't talk to anyone else, Sir. My mother would go mad if it got out I'd been talking like this to anyone.'

Mr Benn stopped what he was doing. 'All right Gordon,' he said. 'I'll have a think about it then. In the meantime, try talking to your sister. Perhaps she will help you. Perhaps she doesn't realise how strongly you feel.'

He tackled Amy before Mum got home.

'About Dad,' he said, eyeballing her.

Amy's mouth set tight, her eyebrows arched. 'I've not got a dad,' she said.

'Oh yes you have. Somewhere.' Gordon said. 'Well, he's *my* dad anyway. The only one I've got.' His chin came up defiantly.

'And he left us. When you were born!' she said.

It felt like she'd hit him.

So.

He'd always know it was *his* fault. Amy knew it. And his mother...

Amy went as if to leave the room. But Gordon grabbed her arm. 'Why was it my fault Amy?' he said desperately.

As Amy turned round and looked at him she looked surprised. 'Don't be silly!' she said. 'It wasn't your fault. How could it have been your fault? Nobody ever said it was *your* fault.'

Gordon was confused. 'But that's how it feels,' he said sadly.

Amy shook her head hard.

He stared at her. 'Well – whatever happened and whose fault it was,' he said slowly, 'I'm going to find him, Amy. So there!'

It was her turn to look as if she'd been hit.

He rushed upstairs.

The next day he reported to Mr Benn. 'It was hopeless, Sir. My sister doesn't want to know.'

'What about grandparents?' Mr Benn said.

'There's Gran,' Gordon said. 'But she's not likely to help me do something my mum's so against.'

'But you never know,' Mr Benn said. 'Tell me about her.'

'Gran lives on her own. Gramps died when I was three. She lives in town. She works in an office there.' He paused. 'I suppose I must have other grandparents somewhere. But I don't know about them.'

Mr Benn ran his hand over his head with a sigh. 'Try your gran, Gordon,' he said. 'You must give her a chance.'

They saw Gran mainly at weekends.

But Gordon didn't usually get a chance to talk to her alone.

Somehow, though, that's what he'd got to do.

So.

He'd have to go to see Gran at work, wouldn't he?

And the Easter holidays were coming up, weren't they?

Chapter Eight

At break on the last day of term, Gordon sauntered up to Sean in the playground.

Sean had his head down, dribbling a stone along the ground.

'This holiday I'm going to find out where my dad is,' Gordon announced.

Sean stopped dribbling the stone. 'Good idea, Gord,' he said.

They wandered round, hands in pockets.

'And how's the new boyfriend?' Gordon asked conversationally. Wondering what it would be like if his mum had boyfriends like Sean's mum did. It would be all right if he was like Eddie, wouldn't it?

'Del Boy's great,' Sean said. 'I really like him. Let's us do what we like. He's been with us two months now.'

'Is that his real name?' Gordon asked.

'Don't be stupid, Gord. It's 'cos he's got this three-wheel-thingummy. Mum loves it. Everybody waves to them when they go out in it. They all call him Del Boy. She says it's cool. So how are you going to find out where your dad is then, Gord?'

'I need your help, Sean.'

Sean began to swagger. 'Anything I can do, Gord,' he said.

'Well in the school holidays Mum's at work. So Amy's in charge.'

Sean pursed his lips. 'That's bad news, Gord. Sisters are more trouble than mums.'

'I'm going to tell her I'm spending the day with you, Sean. Is that all right?'

'Course it is, Gord. No worries. What are the plans then?'

'I'm going to go into town. To see Gran at work.'

'I'd better go with you then,' Sean said. 'My sister can cover for both of us. She's always getting me to fib for her. Make a change for her to do a bit of fibbing for me...'

Both boys knew town well. But not the back streets. They had the street map with them, though, and found the street they wanted, then located Gran's office.

But it was only eleven thirty.

'Gran's lunch break should be around twelve thirty or one o'clock. So we'll have to wait till then,' Gordon said. 'I hope she's there,' he said nervously.

'What's her number?' Sean said and gave Gordon his mobile. Gordon had written the number down and rang it.

'Hello. Bond's Office Equipment. How may I help?' a voice said.

'Is Mrs Hewitt there?' Gordon asked.

'Who should I say is calling?' the voice asked.

So she was there. He mumbled something into the phone, then switched it off and blew a breath out.

To kill time, they walked up and down the same street. Passing and re-passing an Indian takeaway. Which was shut. A gent's hairdressers. Which was empty. A scruffy little café. Which was full. There was a sari shop. Empty. And a flower shop with an assistant making a floral arrangement.

Every few minutes, Gordon checked his watch. Getting colder and hungrier and more fed up by the minute.

How long could an hour take!

Just when he thought it would never pass, it got to twelve thirty.

'That's it. I'll risk it now,' he said.

Sean patted him on the back, then set off for the town arcade, where they'd meet up later. 'Good luck, Gord,' he said. And strutted off.

Gordon pushed the outside door open and went up the flight of stairs in front of him. At the top there was a sort of a landing with a small glass window with a ledge and a buzzer on it. A notice said, 'Reception. Please Buzz.' He pressed the buzzer.

'Yes?'

He cleared his throat. 'Can I talk to Mrs Hewitt, please,' he said.

'Who is it?'

'It's her grandson, Gordon,' he said.

There was a scuffle, then the door opened and Gran appeared.

She looked agitated. 'Gordon?' she said. 'What on earth's the matter? Is it your mother? Amy?'

'No, Gran,' he said quickly. 'They're fine. But it's the school holidays. I thought I'd come and see you.'

He knew it must sound odd, and Gran stared at him. But then her face softened. 'You've timed it well,' she said. 'I'm just going on my lunch break. I'll get my coat and be with you in a tick. There's a little caff up the road. It's a bit of a dive but they do a lovely bacon butty.'

She disappeared, then reappeared with her coat, and slung it loosely round her shoulders. She put an arm round his shoulder. 'You get taller every time I see you,' she said proudly.

It was cosy inside the caff.

'Usual, Helen?' the woman behind the counter said.

'Twice, Marg,' Gran said. 'This is my grandson, Gordon.'

Marg beamed at him. 'Ahh! Come to see his gran. Nice to see a lad taking an interest in his gran. Do you like your bacon crisped to a cinder, same as her? Can't bear a bit of fat on hers, your gran.'

Gordon nodded. 'The crispier the better,' he said.

'Ahh!' Marg said. 'Go and get comfy then. I'll bring them over.'

'So—' Gran said when they'd sat down. 'To what do I owe the honour?' The worried expression reappeared on her face.

There was no point beating about the bush. 'It's about my dad, Gran.' he blurted out.

Gran sighed. Nodded her head slowly. 'I knew you'd ask one day,' she said. 'But why now, Gordon? Has Maggie heard from him or something after all this time?'

'That's the point, Gran' he said sadly. 'We *never* hear from him, do we?'

Gran's eyes dropped to the table.

'Gran,' he said firmly. 'I need to know about my dad. And you've got to tell me!'

Gran folded her arms and laid them on the table. Then she leaned on them and looked at him… 'And just *what* do you need to know, Gordon?' she said.

Gordon sighed with relief. 'Everything,' he said. 'For a start, I'd like to know where he is – *exactly* – I mean – because I'm going to write to him.' His eyes searched Gran's face as he spoke but for now all she did was listen. 'Then I want to know why he left us. And why he never kept in touch with us. *And* why he hates us. Especially me.'

Gran's eyes clouded. 'I told her,' she said.

Gordon's heart missed a beat.

'I told her to be more open with you,' Gran sighed. 'But she always said the less you knew, the less you'd be hurt too.' She shook her head sadly. 'But I always thought it would backfire. You're obviously hurting now, Gordon.'

All Gordon could do was nod his head.

Gran straightened up. 'Well. To answer one of your questions. I'm afraid I haven't got an address for him.' She lowered her eyes. 'He's not been in touch in years.' She paused. 'And I still think it's your mum you should be talking to, Gordon. Not me,' she said.

'But I've tried, Gran. And it doesn't work.'

Gordon heard his voice rising.

Gran's hand crept across the table top till it rested on top of his. 'If it were up to me...' she said.

'But it is up to you, Gran.' His voice was even higher now. 'Because there's no one else, and it's driving me crazy!'

Gran suddenly looked angry too. Her eyes blazed.

Here we go, Gordon thought. She's mad at me now. She's going to clam up on me too.

But she didn't.

She straightened her back even more. 'Right. Well it *is* up to me then, isn't it, Gordon?' she said. 'Because you have a right to know what happened.' She squeezed his hand. 'Every right.'

He could have hugged her. Instead he managed a watery smile.

The bacon butties arrived, and Marg smiled at them. 'Having a nice little chat are we?' she said.

Every so often as they ate, Gordon caught Gran's eye, and they smiled secretively at each other. It was the best bacon butty he'd ever tasted. Then Gran looked at her watch. 'Back to the grind,' she said.

Gordon's heart missed a beat. Was that it then? But she couldn't leave it there! He grabbed her hand.

'It's all right, Gordon,' she said. 'What about if I was to ask you over on Saturday? You could stay overnight? We could talk properly then.'

Chapter Nine

On the way to the arcade to meet Sean it felt like Gordon couldn't stop grinning. Things were not going to be the same from today.

He found Sean in the arcade. 'I'm on a winning streak, Gord,' he called. 'Can't go yet.' He moved to another machine.

In the end Gordon had to drag him away. 'There's only one bus home and we've got to catch it,' he said.

As soon as they left the arcade, Sean returned to his normal self. 'Mission accomplished, then?' he asked.

Gordon grinned. 'Went like a dream,' he said.

'Where is he, then?'

'Don't be stupid, Sean. It was never going to be that easy. But at least I've cracked it.'

He explained everything to Sean. 'Your gran sounds cool, Gordon,' he said.

'Yes. She is,' Gordon said warmly. 'What's your gran like, Sean?'

'Nan? She's another nutter. Like Mum,' Sean said matter-of-factly.

When he got home, Gordon sauntered into the house. Ready with the lies. But the house was quiet. He guessed that Amy was upstairs, and bounded up two at a time, alerting her to his return.

But when he got to her door he hesitated. When Amy was in her room, you disturbed her at your own risk. He heard her latest favourite CD playing quietly in the background and knocked. 'I'm home,' he called.

The music stopped. Paper rustled. Then Amy appeared at the door. Hollow-eyed. Overdosing on revision for her GCSEs Gordon supposed. She didn't even ask him where he'd been all day, or what he'd been up to.

So much for the lies.

Still. There were plenty more where they'd come from!

Gran had told him she'd ring that night, so he was on tenterhooks all evening. And when the phone finally rang, Mum got there first. 'Hello, Mum. All right?' she said. 'Um – right...'

Gordon wondered what Gran was saying.

'Just a mo, Mum, I'll ask him,' Mum put her hand over the phone and looked at him from under raised eyebrows. 'Gran wants to know if you'd like to go and see her at the weekend, Gordon? Says you can stay over?'

'Tell her I'm busy revising,' Amy said.

'I think she only means Gordon—' Mum said, looking curious.

'OK,' Gordon said as if it was the most natural thing in the world.

Mum frowned. 'Sure? You don't have to stay over—'

'No. That's OK Mum. It's fine.' he said.

Mum shrugged. 'He says that's OK, Mum. Right... Yes... See you Saturday, then. Bye.'

She put the phone down.

'*Bonding* with her favourite grandson, indeed!' She laughed. 'What next? *And* she's getting a video out for the pair of you. Goodness knows what it'll be, Gordon.'

'I bet she's never seen the inside of a video shop,' Amy said.

'It'll be a laugh,' Gordon said defensively, wanting to stick up for Gran, but afraid he'd give something away. 'I'll explain the bits to her she doesn't understand,' he said and laughed.

'You're both full of surprises and that's for sure,'

Mum said. 'To be honest, I didn't think you'd want to go.'

'Gran's all right,' Gordon muttered.

And that was that.

When Gran picked him up on Saturday afternoon, Gordon wondered what would come of it.

As he got in the car with his overnight bag, he thought Mum had a strange look on her face. Was it just curiosity? Or could it be suspicion?

Gordon felt guilty...

'I think your mum's a bit confused,' Gran said as they pulled away.

When they got to her little town house, they had tea and he helped Gran clear the table. Then she disappeared.

When she came back she had an armful of photograph albums.

He hadn't seen them for ages, and it took his breath away just seeing them.

'I'm going to clear up in the kitchen,' Gran said and left him alone with them.

They were neatly numbered.

He reached for the first one. It was different to the rest. The wedding album.

He breathed deeply. Felt the smoothness of the cover. Clutched the album to him, before opening it.

And there he was.

It was a picture of the groom. And no mistaking him. Because the eyes staring out at him were not the eyes of a stranger. In fact they were so familiar that it was like looking in a mirror.

It struck Gordon then how painful this must be for his mum. It must be like looking at *him* and being reminded every day...

He drew his finger round the outline of his father's face as if he could feel the skin. Scrutinised every part of him.

Turned the page. Groom and best man.

He turned over again. And there she was. The bride.

He was looking at a mother he didn't know any more than he knew his father. Because he'd never seen Mum with this look on her face. It was a look of such happiness that it leapt off the page.

He began to flip through the pages now. Serious photos. Casual ones. The two of them together.

Kissing!

Gordon smiled happily. Pleased to see that there'd been a time when they *were* happy. A time when she'd loved him and he'd loved her.

He opened the next album. The year of Amy's birth. And there she was. With proud parents.

But when he eventually arrived at the one of his birth, everything was different. No sign of the happy couple any more. Just his mother. And Amy. And him. And the expression on his mother's face that he was so familiar with. Where the light had gone out of her eyes.

He browsed through all of the albums now, flicking backwards and forwards, page after page after page. Ending up back at the beginning. The wedding album. But this time studying the groups. Looking for clues. Seeing Gramps, who he just remembered. Like Amy must remember their dad. Then searching for his other grandparents. That other family.

They were there. But they could be anybody. They were complete strangers.

He laid his arms on the table and dropped his head down.

He felt Gran's arms creep round him. 'I'm so sorry, Gordon,' she said.

Chapter Ten

Gran reached for the wedding album and opened it at the photograph of his father on his own. She stared at it for a minute then began to talk.

'Your father was – is – very good looking,' she said.

That meant *he* was too, Gordon thought in passing.

'Your mum fell for him straight away. It was "Phil this," and "Phil that". We liked him too, your Gramps and me. Though we weren't sure whether he was the right one for our daughter. She was all we had, Gordon. And we wanted the world for her.'

Gran paused. As if gathering strength. 'When she said they wanted to get engaged and married, we worried for them. She was so young. Twenty, but immature, while Phil was twenty-five, and streetwise. He'd been around a bit you see, Gordon. Anyway. They were going to get married whether we liked it or not.' She sighed. '"Give it more time," your Gramps told her. But she could always twist him round her little finger.'

Gran turned the pages, then smoothed her hand round the edge of the photograph where his mother and father only had eyes for each other. 'It was a lovely wedding, though. A very happy day, Gordon.'

It made Gordon happy to hear that.

'But they were like so many young couples at that time,' she said and her voice broke. 'They got caught up in an expensive mortgage and a car and washing machines. Wanted the lot. And it meant debts. Not like in our day,' she added. 'Your Gramps and me never got into debt. Always paid for what we had. It was like that in our day. But then it all changed. And not for the better. Because just when they made it so easy for young couples to get everything and pay later, the jobs let them down.' Gran shuddered. 'He was made redundant. One time after another. He just got settled into another job when it happened again. And by this time they had Amy and your Mum wasn't working either.'

There was a long silence.

'That's when the real trouble began,' she added.

Gordon waited.

'Your dad started going out.'

Gran's face was full of misery.

The way she'd told it made it sound like a history lesson. It could be anybody she was talking about. Except this was his family. It felt like Gordon couldn't get any sadder, but he wanted to know the rest. 'Go on Gran,' he said urgently.

'Then there was another baby on the way.' Gran paused. Looked at him.

'*Me*,' he said.

Gran nodded. 'And then—'

This time there was a pause which went on for ever. And when he looked at her, Gran's eyes reflected the sadness that was now dragging at Gordon's insides too.

'So what happened, Gran?' he whispered.

Needing to know how it ended.

But in the end having to break the silence himself.

'What did he do Gran?' he said, an edge creeping into his voice.

'He found someone else, didn't he?' Gran whispered.

Gordon was devastated.

Gran reached for his hand and held it tight. 'And then he got the job,' she said. 'Good money. And good prospects.' She sighed. 'And in Canada.'

Gordon dropped his head into his hands. And when he felt Gran's arms round his shoulders, his shoulders sagged.

Gran eventually got up and wandered round the room. Blowing specks of dust off this ornament and that. 'So he went. He went to Canada. With her...' Her voice trailed off.

'And forgot about us!' Gordon said, feeling himself sweating as if he'd run a mile. His palms were wet. His forehead clammy.

'No. He wrote at first—' Gran muttered.

Gordon breathed heavily.

Gran cleared her throat.

'He asked for photos, Gordon. Especially of you. Because he'd never seen you. But Amy as well. His "little pumpkin" that's what he called her.'

And what would he have called him, then?

'But your mum returned all the letters to him unopened. And in the end he gave up writing. Just sent a final letter asking her for a divorce and telling us he was going to marry *her*.' She headed for the door. 'I'll make us some drinking chocolate,' she said.

But they *had* loved each other once, was all Gordon could think.

And took comfort from it. He clasped his hands between his knees and rocked gently.

And his father *had* written.

Gran came in carrying mugs of steaming hot chocolate. She put his down. Drank hers, cradling the mug in her hands the way Mum told him not to do.

'Mum should have told me he wrote,' Gordon said.

Gran put her mug down and got an envelope out of her pocket. Gave it to Gordon. 'This is the last letter we had from him,' she said. 'He sent it to us.'

Gordon opened and read the crumpled airmail letter, addressed to Gran and Gramps.

Dear Grace and Bob,
How are you both?
Maggie just returns my letters. She won't tell me
how the kids are. So could you?
Could you send me a photo of my little boy
please? And my little pumpkin. She'll be getting
bigger and prettier by the day.
I'm asking Maggie for a divorce and getting
remarried. We're moving upstate.
Please don't think too badly of me.
Phil.

Gordon gulped.

'And did you?' he asked. 'Did you write back to him? Did you send him a photo of me and Amy?'

She nodded her head. 'I did,' she said. 'But we never heard from him again.'

Her sigh echoed Gordon's.

'Amy took it very badly,' Gran continued. 'She adored her daddy. And when he disappeared she didn't understand. She was too little. She was old enough to miss him, though. She asked for him everyday. And she changed from being a normal happy little girl into a troubled sad one. And that made Maggie even more bitter.'

Gran looked at Gordon thoughtfully.

'And has talking about it made things better or

worse, Gordon?' she asked him. 'Because that's what your mother's silence is all about you know. Her need to protect you. To stop you being hurt.'

And it had done just the opposite! Gordon thought.

But at least he knew everything now. He'd even read a letter from his father.

So how *did* he feel now, knowing that his father had betrayed all of them?

Well.

Bad as it was, it still felt better *knowing*.

'At least I know my dad loved Mum once, Gran,' he said fiercely. 'And he loved me. I'm still going to find him.'

'That's my boy,' she said and gave a weak smile.

That night in bed he thought about Gran. It must have been awful for her as well, he thought.

Awful for everybody.

The Perfect Imperfect.

Chapter Eleven

When he got home, Gordon badly wanted to talk to both or either Mum or Amy. But every time he tried, something dried up inside him.

So, for now, he kept his peace. Promising himself that on Monday, the beginning of a new term, he would talk to Mr Benn. Knowing that he would help.

He explained to Mr Benn everything that had happened in the holiday. Then added, simply, 'So I'm going to find my dad and write to him, somehow, Sir.'

'Right,' Mr Benn said, chewing his lip. 'Right.'

Mr Benn didn't look or sound very sure of himself. And it wasn't the reaction Gordon had expected. 'So how do I go about it now, Sir?' he said, drumming his fingers impatiently on the table.

'It's difficult,' Mr Benn said cautiously.

For heaven's sake! As if he didn't know that, Gordon thought.

'You *must* discuss it with your mother, Gordon,' Mr Benn said. Avoiding Gordon's eyes. 'I can arrange a meeting here at school if you like. Neutral territory and all that. I can sit in on it.'

'It's not a Drama lesson!' Gordon yelled. Then apologised. 'Sorry, Sir.'

'No. That's all right, Gordon. But—'

Gordon noticed he was chewing his lip again.

'—I think it's time to call in the professionals,' he finally blurted out.

Gordon opened his eyes wide. 'And who might they be?' he said accusingly. It was bad enough involving Mr Benn. But Mum would never forgive him for calling in the *professionals* too, whoever they were.

It was beginning to sound like a soap on TV.

'They're family mediators, Gordon. And they're trained for this sort of thing,' Mr Benn was saying. He ran his hand over his head with a frown.

This wasn't the full-on Mr Benn Gordon was used to and he was disappointed.

But Mr Benn looked him in the eye at last. 'We could be a bit out of our depth, Gordon,' he said apologetically. 'And I don't want to make things worse. I want the help you get to be the best help.

The right help. And I'm not sure I'm the person for that any more...' he dropped his eyes again.

'Right,' Gordon said. It was his turn now. 'Right!' he repeated. And got up. He stalked round the room. Hands in pockets. Shoulders hunched. Eyes narrowed. Working himself up to give Mr Benn the earful he deserved.

Except that he could actually see where he was coming from.

He stopped prowling, and with his back to Mr Benn, lowered his head. Well. He might go along with a meeting with Mum. Here. If he could get her here. But he drew the line at *professionals*.

He came and sat down opposite Mr Benn.

'Right!' he said.

'That's three times,' Mr Benn said, a grin hovering on his face. 'So what exactly *is* right?'

'Talking to my mum. Here. With you. OK. But no professionals.'

Mr Benn sat back and folded his arms. 'Right!' he said.

They both laughed.

Gordon decided to broach the subject with Amy first, and tackled her as soon as he got home.

'Amy,' he said casually. 'About Dad.'

Amy grabbed her books and made for the stairs.

But Gordon was faster. He slipped in front of her. Barring the way. 'About our father!' he repeated fiercely.

'I'm going upstairs,' she said, pushing past him.

He chased after her. 'No you're not,' he said. Leaping in front of her again.

Her eyes blazed. 'I am not going to talk to you about ... *him*. I don't want to talk about *him*,' she said.

'But I want to talk to *you* about *him*,' Gordon said furiously.

Amy pushed him aside. 'Get out of my way,' she said, and ran into her room. She slammed the door.

'Well somebody's got to talk to me,' Gordon yelled. 'Because Mr Benn says so.'

Her door opened again and she stared at him blankly.

'Mr Benn says we've got to discuss it. I've got rights,' he said. 'And Gran agrees,' he added defiantly.

Amy looked incredulous. 'Why, Gordon?' she said. 'When you've got such a pig for a father, why do you want to go chasing after him?'

Gordon sat down on the top of the stairs. 'I just want the chance to know him Amy. Like you knew him once.'

'But that only makes it worse. Can't you see that?'

Amy said quietly. She ran back into her room.

Gordon was shaking as he went downstairs. But he wasn't finished yet. Now he was started, he was determined to see it through.

'Where's everybody?' Mum said, bustling in, 'Oh.

There you are, Gordon.
It was so quiet I thought no one was in.'
Gordon didn't say anything.

She frowned at him. 'Is something the matter,
Gordon? Has something happened at school?' A
nervous edge crept into her voice.

'You mean apart from me getting into trouble for
not concentrating these days,' he said, then quickly
added, 'Mr Benn says...' and dried up. He tried again
– hesitantly – 'Mr Benn's going to contact you, Mum –
about us going up to school – to discuss my father.'

There. He'd said it.

And it was just as he expected. His mother's mouth

set. Her chin came up. Her eyes darted. 'I hope you're making this up, Gordon,' she said, the words short and clipped.

'No. No I'm not, actually.' Gordon was fired up now too. 'You see, I've talked to Mr Benn. And Gran. And they both back me. I'm going to find my dad, Mum!' he said firmly.

Mum went to the phone and dialled Gran's number.

Chapter Twelve

It sounded like a heated exchange.

Eventually Mum put the phone down and flopped onto the settee.

Gordon could see she was upset and he felt terrible. He sat down next to her. '*Mum*,' he said.

Then she began to cry.

Amy appeared. 'Mum!' She looked appalled. 'What have you said to her, Gordon?'

Gordon slouched upstairs.

When he eventually came back downstairs Mum acted as if nothing had happened.

For Gordon, this was worse than the tears. Because if she thought he was going to forget about it, she was wrong.

He ate his tea as fast as he could so he could go round Sean's.

Anything to get out of the house...

'It's no good,' he told Sean miserably.

'What are you on about, Gord?' Sean asked.

Gordon told him what he'd said to his mother. Her reaction. Her crying.

'Don't let that put you off, Gord,' Sean said. He clicked his teeth.

Gordon couldn't help laughing. 'You sound as if you're the expert on that sort of thing.'

Sean preened himself. 'You'd be an expert if you lived in this house,' he said.

His mother, who'd just come into the room, clipped him over the ear affectionately. 'Less of that, my son,' she said. 'Boys' talk is it?' She giggled. 'You want me out of the way, then.' She left them to it.

'So. What now, Sean?' Gordon said.

'Well. There must be somebody else can help apart from your gran,' Sean said.

Gordon hadn't told Sean anything about Mr Benn. After all, teacher's pet would be even worse than mummy's boy, wouldn't it?

'There must be someone else knew your dad, Gord,' Sean said.

Good point, Gordon thought.

And a photograph came to mind.

The two of them posing together – smart – buttonholes and everything – smiling.

Groom and best man.

'Dad's best man!' he said to Sean excitedly.

'There you are Gord. You must know him if he was your dad's best friend.'

'No. I've never seen him in my life,' Gordon said.

So how to track *him* down then? He breathed heavily. Bit his lip. Was anything straightforward?

'Everyone I know comes from around here, though,' he said, thinking aloud. 'Mum. My dad. Gran and Gramps. So I should think his best friend lived around here too – perhaps Gran knows him, Sean!'

'Good thinking Gord.'

'Can I use your mobile, Sean? I'll give you the money—' he asked. Wondering when, if ever, he'd get one of his own.

Sean handed his over.

He rang Gran.

'Hello, Gordon. How are things?' she asked.

He explained.

'She's going to make herself ill,' Gran sighed down the phone.

Gordon could hear the worry in her voice. 'I know,' he agreed. 'But I've thought of something,' he said.

'Sounds intriguing,' she said. 'Tell me.'

'Dad's best man – if I could find him he'd probably still be in touch with my dad. Do you know his name, Gran? Do you know where he lives? If I can find *him*—' he said breathlessly.

'Steady on Gordon,' Gran said. 'But that's a good idea. Now let me think. His name was Gary. Gary Grey.' Her voice became more animated. 'And he lived somewhere around here.'

'Wicked!' Gordon said.

'Mind, I don't know where. And I've not seen him, or heard from him in years,' Gran warned.

'So! I'll go through the phone book,' Gordon said. 'If he still lives round here I'll find him Gran.'

'Good luck, my love,' she said. 'And let me know if – when – you get a result. But Gordon,' her voice was suddenly intense. 'Go easy on your mother. She can't help how she feels. She'll come round in the end though. You'll see...'

They got the phone directory out and found the Greys.

Hundreds of them!

Gordon was dismayed. After counting the first hundred he stopped counting and estimated that there was at least another hundred, possibly more.

But it would take for ever to ring round all of them – and what about the cost? He tried to work out mentally what the cost would be. He'd raid his savings anyway. He'd get the money from somewhere.

'Sean,' he said. 'I need another big favour. I know it'll cost. But you won't be out of pocket,' he wheedled.

Sean said he'd just bought a ten pound *pay as you go* card for his mobile. And agreed to help as long as Gordon replaced it. And another if necessary. But as it was getting late now, they put it off till the next day after school.

Next day, he told Mr Benn the meeting with Mum was off. Mr Benn was concerned. 'But it's all right, Sir,' Gordon said quickly. 'I've got another plan.'

He told him about Gary Grey. Mr Benn wished him luck.

After school no one else was in at Sean's.

They got the phone directory.

Not for the first time, Gordon thought what a funny thing names were. If Gary Grey's surname had been Grickos or Grioble – he spotted just one of each in the directory – the job would have been easy. And cheap. Whereas a name like Grey made it almost impossible. And expensive! Then he wondered about the name itself. Where it came from, and why it was so popular.

'At least he's not called Smith!' he said to Sean. He'd already checked the Smiths out to cheer himself up. There were pages of them.

'Well, we'd better get on with it then,' Sean said.

Gordon made the calls. Sean ticked them off – or marked them if there was no response – for calling back later.

'Hello,' Gordon said every time. 'I'm trying to trace Gary Grey. Have I got the right number?'

By the time he came to the end of the first column it had become like a mantra.

At the end of the second column it was getting tedious.

At the end of the third, it was soul-destroying.

'I can't believe so many people have the same name!' Gordon declared. 'And all in this one area. Think of how many Greys there must be in the whole country – the world!' he added bleakly – as if it might come to that.

Some people at the end of the phone were quite rude. But most were friendly. And some wanted to be helpful – these were the ones who went through their family history trying to track a Gary down, then said they'd heard of a Gary Grey who used to live a few houses down but had moved recently and no, they were sorry, but they didn't have a forwarding address.

Gordon's voice was getting flatter and flatter.

Suddenly no one on the other end seemed friendly or helpful.

But he persevered to the end.

'That's the lot, for now! ' he finally said and threw the directory onto the floor. 'I'll have to come back later, Sean, when people are home from work. I'll think of an excuse. And thanks again for the use of your mobile,' he said sheepishly.

He went back to Sean's later, telling them that he was going to do his homework.

This time, as Sean's mum and sister were both in, Gordon and Sean went up to Sean's bedroom.

And this time, there was a response from nearly every number.

And eventually they got the answer they were hoping for!

When Gordon asked, 'Is Gary Grey there, please?' a child's voice answered, 'Do you mean my dad?'

Gordon's back stiffened. 'Yes. I think so,' he said and laughed. He put his thumb up to Sean, who punched the air. 'Can I speak to him?' Gordon said breathlessly.

'*Mum*,' the voice yelled.

'Hello,' a woman's voice said. 'Who is this?'

Gordon said, 'My name's Gordon Black. I'm trying to find Gary Grey. He was my dad's best man.'

'Gordon Black? *Phil Black*'s boy?' she exclaimed. 'Blow me down! Yes. Gary was Phil's best man.'

It was like an electric shock going through Gordon. His palms went damp. He nearly dropped the phone. Then his mouth went dry and his throat felt like there was something blocking it.

'Gary was sick with worry about what happened to your family,' the woman was saying. '"It's such a tragedy!" he says even now.'

'Have you got his address? I want his address,' Gordon heard himself say. His voice sounded peculiar even to himself, but he managed to get the words out somehow.

There was a silence.

'Are you still there, Mrs Grey?' he asked anxiously.

'Yes, Gordon.'

'Do you still hear from him?' Gordon said. Trying to sound normal. 'I was hoping you'd have his address...'

Paper and pencil were to the ready.

She told him they used to send Christmas cards regularly. But they hadn't heard for the last year or so – 'Let me give you the last address we had anyway, Gordon. Just a mo—' she said.

He wrote down the address.

Chapter Thirteen

Back at home he had paper ready and waiting.

He picked up the pen. But then didn't know what to write – because the thought that these could be the words his dad might actually read, blew his mind.

Dear Dad, he finally wrote.

And just seeing the words made his hand tremble and the words dry up – because words couldn't actually express how he felt, could they? The excitement – excitement that the words might find his dad. The fear – fear that they'd never reach him. Fear that if they did, he wouldn't be interested. Fear that he'd never reply. Excitement that he would!

Gordon looked round his room in quiet desperation. Then stared at the sheet of paper again. Because, actually, words were all he had.

He picked up the pen again, looked at the words *Dear Dad* again. Breathed deeply. Then blew hot angry breath out of his lungs.

And that was when *Brad* came into his head. Because Brad would – well – Brad would just get on with it – wouldn't he?

Gordon gave a sharp little shrug and wrote, *Dear Dad, I'm Gordon, your son.* He heard Brad's voice mocking him – (That's pretty obvious isn't it? Think STYLE, Man. STYLE!)

He screwed the sheet up. Got another one.

Dear Dad, he wrote again. *Hi! It's Gordon. I'm thirteen. And though I've never seen you I often think about you.* (That should hit him hard, Gord! I like that. That's STYLE). *I've always had a good idea what you look like, though, because I look like you – that's what Mum says, anyway. I don't know you, Dad,* (Cool Gord! Hit him where it hurts!) *but I would like to know you. Very much.* Gordon-The-Bold. For once in his life it felt like his name suited him perfectly. *So will you write to me?* he finally added.

And felt as if he'd run a marathon. Not that he'd ever run a marathon. But he was sure if he had, this is how he'd feel.

He re-read the letter out aloud. Trying and testing it. Weighing the words.

Gordon so wanted it to be right.

> *Dear Dad,*
> *It's Gordon. I'm thirteen now. And though I've never seen you I often think about you. I've always had a good idea what you look like, though, because I look like you – that's what Mum says, anyway. I don't know you, Dad, but I would like to know you. Very much. So will you write to me?*

But how to finish?

In the end he wrote, *Looking forward to hearing from you*, and signed his name self-consciously, *Gordon*.

He put the letter in an envelope, and sealed it.

At school, he saw Mr Benn in the corridor and told him what he'd done.

Mr Benn looked at him. 'Well. You could have quite a wait for a reply. So try to forget about it now – and concentrate on your work Gordon – something you've not been doing much of lately.' Mr Benn lowered his chin and looked at Gordon from under lowered eyes. 'There's end of year tests coming up soon,' he said slowly.

Gordon scowled. At the moment he couldn't care less about end of term tests.

Mr Benn looked disapproving. 'Don't let this spoil you, Gordon,' he said. 'I don't want you going off the rails like someone else we both know.'

It was good advice. But difficult to follow.

Every night he dreamed about his dad getting the letter.

Every morning, he dreamed that there'd be a reply from him.

And every day he was disappointed when there wasn't.

He'd had to give his dad Sean's address, in case Mum got hold of the letter and kept it from him. And every day his insides did a flip when he saw Sean.

So when one day, soon after he'd got home from school, Sean came round with it, he went numb with shock.

Chapter Fourteen

Gordon rushed outside with Sean.

Sean wanted Gordon to open the letter there and then, but Gordon was adamant. 'I'll open it on my own, Sean,' he said.

'But that's not fair, Gord— ' Sean started to say.

But Gordon didn't have the energy to explain. 'Too bad!' he said in a strangled voice. Then he shot back inside.

He wasn't sharing this with anybody.

Amy was in the kitchen cutting a hunk of bread. As he watched her spread butter and jam on it he felt himself heave.

Amy looked at him. 'What's the matter?' she said. And her face was concerned. 'You look awful, Gordie,' she said.

Gordon couldn't remember the last time she'd called him by the pet name and it made him feel worse.

Amy looked more concerned. 'What's up?' she asked.

'I'm OK,' he said, clearing his throat. 'I'm fine. Too hot. That's all.'

Amy got some juice out of the fridge and poured some for him.

'Thanks,' he said. Longing to be upstairs. If his sister knew what was in his pocket she'd kill him!

Amy took a bite of bread and headed upstairs herself.

Gordon slipped up after her, and shut his door.

He leaned on it and took some deep breaths. Then dragged the letter out of his pocket.

It was addressed to *Gordon Black*, c/o *Sean Taylor*.

Had his father guessed why this was necessary, he wondered?

He turned it over and noticed the address from *sender* wasn't the address he'd sent the letter to. Which probably explained the long wait for a reply.

Things were looking good.

His teeth were chattering now.

Gordon-the-wimp!

Then a voice penetrated the panic. '*Come on Gordon-the-bold.*' It was Brad's voice.

Gordon strode round the room a few times, pumping himself up, then gripped the letter firmly. Next thing it was open.

Dear Gordon, son, – the words blurred –
I can't believe you did this, son – That word again. Gordon couldn't get enough of it – *Wrote to me, after all this time I mean. To get a letter from you – I don't mind admitting, I had a few tears. I wrote so many letters to your mother but she returned them all unopened. I'd love us to get to know each other too, son. So I'm following your lead and forwarding to you and Amy airline tickets to come and see me in the summer holidays.*
I've always loved you both – and always will.
By the way, you have two half-sisters here. Janine and Freya. Six and five. (God – more women Gordon thought.)
Amy's old enough to accompany you on a long haul flight, and the airlines are wonderful with kids anyway. It would please me more than I can possibly say, Gordon, to have you come and spend some time with me.
Looking forward to you saying – Yes!
Love you lots,
Dad.

Love you lots! His father loved him and wanted to get to know him – and he was going to get the chance to do just that.

Gordon punched his fist in the air.

Yessss! he yelled at the top of his voice.

Amy rushed into his room. 'God, Gordon! You scared me. What's the matter with you today?' she yelled.

Gordon tried to push the letter in his pocket, but Amy saw it.

'Who's sending you an airmail letter?' she asked with a suspicious frown.

Gordon bit his lip.

Her frown deepened. Her eyes narrowed. 'No!' she whispered. Then grabbed him and pulled the letter out of his pocket.

'It's mine! Give it here,' Gordon screamed.

Mum appeared in the doorway.

'What on earth is going on?' she demanded.

Amy waved the letter at her.

'No!' Mum said in a shocked voice.

'I think it is!' Amy said.

'Gordon!' Mum said.

'Yes it is a letter from *him*,' Gordon yelled in a rage. 'And you're not returning this one unopened!

It's mine. Give it here Amy.'

But Amy gave the letter to their mother.

She opened the envelope, and the airline tickets fluttered out of it.

'And what are these?' she said.

'What do they look like?' Gordon shouted. 'They're airline tickets for me and Amy to go to Canada. And if Amy doesn't go with me, I'll go on my own. No one's stopping me.'

'Oh no? We'll see about that,' his mother said, and put the tickets in her pocket.

Chapter Fifteen

Gordon raced down the stairs and out of the house.

He'd had enough of his mother and his sister.

Enough of everything.

He had to get away.

But where to go?

Sean's house wasn't far enough away.

He could cycle to Gran's, but she'd tell Mum where he was for sure.

The Wilkinsons? Ellie was Mum's friend. She'd do the same.

That only left one person...

He knew where Mr Benn lived, he'd been to rehearsals there. So he got out his bike and cycled there.

Mr Benn's battered old Renault 4 was parked outside.

Gordon pushed his bike inside the front gate and rang the bell.

Mr Benn answered the door. 'Gordon!' he said.

'I've left home!' Gordon announced.

Mr Benn's face fell.

'You've got to tell me what to do. Where to go. Can I stay here tonight?' Gordon said.

Mr Benn shook his head. 'Certainly not,' he said firmly.

That shook Gordon's confidence. 'So where can I go, then?' he shouted.

'You'd better come in and tell me what's happened, Gordon.'

Gordon looked round Mr Benn's flat. At the debris on the floor – the remains of more than today's takeaway, that was for sure. The room smelt like a tip in hot weather.

'I wasn't expecting visitors,' Mr Benn said sheepishly.

'I've had enough of my mum and my sister!' Gordon yelled.

'Stop talking like Brad,' Mr Benn said.

But Gordon was proud to be talking like Brad.

'Gordon,' Mr Benn said firmly. 'Whatever's happened can be sorted out. There's no need for this.'

'No, it can't be sorted out,' Gordon snapped. 'My dad sent me tickets to got to Canada. But she won't let me go. She's got the tickets.'

Mr Benn pointed to the door. 'Out!' he said.

Gordon found himself being bundled out again. Mr Benn came too. 'Where are we going?' Gordon demanded.

'Where do you think?' Mr Benn said.

'I'm not going home!' Gordon yelled.

'Yes you are!' Mr Benn shouted. 'We're going to sort this out once and for all.'

Mr Benn wheeled Gordon's bike into the hall. 'It can stay here for tonight,' he said. Then they got into Mr Benn's car.

When Mum saw Mr Benn with Gordon she looked – uncomfortable.

'Can we talk, Mrs Black?' Mr Benn said.

'I – don't – think – so,' she said through clenched teeth.

'I told you, Sir!' Gordon yelled.

Amy, who was lurking in the background, looked excruciatingly embarrassed.

'Gordon had no right to do what's he's done behind my back,' his mum said. But then she motioned Mr Benn to sit down. And sat down on the edge of a chair herself.

Gordon stood to attention stiffly.

'I'm sorry, Mrs Black,' Mr Benn said. 'But Gordon has been extremely upset for some time now.'

Mum frowned, but listened as he continued.

'His school work is suffering. I think you'll find that his results at the end of term will bear witness to that fact, Mrs Black,' he said deliberately.

Clever! Gordon thought. But at the same time, it occurred to him that what Mr Benn was saying was true. For the first time in his life, Gordon hadn't been doing his best at school. And, he realised, it wasn't a

very nice feeling. He dropped his eyes.

'Gordon came to me for help some time ago Mrs Black. But he insisted it went no farther than me. And I agreed to respect that. But it's gone beyond that now. And it needs sorting. Gordon has rights in this matter too, you know.'

Gordon looked up again. That was even better!

His mother's shoulders suddenly slumped and her face crumpled.

'There's people could help. Family mediation—' Mr Benn said less brusquely.

But Mum shook her head firmly. 'No,' she gasped.

'It would help, Mrs Black,' Mr Benn persisted.

'Everything would be given an airing. Everything brought out in the open in an impartial setting with impartial people.'

His mother shook her head fiercely.

'But I only want to see my dad!' Gordon cried.

Then remembered the tickets.

'I want my airline ticket,' he shouted at Mum.

'And what are you going to do with it? You know how we feel about it!' Amy spluttered.

Mr Benn sighed. 'But do you know how *Gordon* feels, Amy?' he said gently.

His words cut through the conversation.

'Course we do. We've always known how *he* feels,' Amy said.

'I suggest that you don't really know, Amy. When you consider Gordon's feelings it's always in the context of your own – not his. Gordon only wants to get to know his father. Every child has a right to do that.'

Nobody spoke for a while.

Then his mother slumped back in the chair.

For one awful moment Gordon thought she was going to cry.

But then she looked at Gordon. 'You're right,' she eventually said.

'Excuse me?' Gordon said.

'You're right!' his mother said. 'You must go, Gordon.'

She fumbled in her pocket and got the tickets out then handed them to Gordon.

Gordon held them tight. 'Do you mean it, Mum? Can I go? Can I really go? Thanks Mum. Thanks!' he gasped.

'Well. *I'm* not going anywhere,' Amy said, tight-lipped, and she rushed out of the room...

Gordon was ecstatic. When Mr Benn had gone, he rang Gran and told her the good news. 'Well done, Gordon. You did it!' she said.

But when she visited them on Saturday, Gran was more cautious.

'So, Maggie?' she said.

'So!' Mum said. And the next thing, something bubbled up inside her and she was crying. Again.

Gran put her arms round Mum and hugged her fiercely. 'It's going to be all right, Maggie,' she said.

'See what you've done,' Amy said.

Gordon went upstairs and left them to it.

Gran eventually found her way up to his bedroom. She sat on the edge of the bed.

'Don't look so glum, my pet,' she said. 'It is all right, you know. Your mum knows she's in the wrong.'

Gordon nodded.

'It's funny how close laughter and tears can be,' Gran murmured, sniffing. 'It's the same with love and hate.'

'Does Mum really hate Dad, Gran?'

'I don't know. Probably not any more. But she's very sad about how it all turned out,' Gran said. 'And I'd like to bet that some of Amy's tears are because her feelings are not quite so cut and dried as she makes out they are.'

They heard Amy moving around next door. 'I'm going to talk to Amy now, Gordon. You go down and talk to your mum,' Gran said.

He sat down next to her and Mum looked at him. 'Sorry, love,' she said quietly.

'It's OK, Mum,' he said.

'No, it isn't Gordon. All this time trying to protect you – thinking it was for your own good – and I've only made things worse, haven't I? I'm so very sorry.'

He put his arms round her. 'So you don't mind me going to Canada, then?' he whispered.

She sighed. 'I mind. I mind terribly. But you must go,' she said.

This time it was Mum wrote to Dad. She showed Gordon the letter.

Brief. But to the point.

Phil,
Gordon is looking forward to coming to see you.
Amy isn't coming, but we'll make sure Gordon is
looked after on the flight. As long as you do your
bit the other end.
Look after him.
Maggie.

Dear Maggie, he replied.
Amy might change her mind. If she does I'll look
after them well. But anyway, don't worry about a
thing.
Thank you.
Phil.

'Canada,' Sean said. 'You lucky so and so! Couldn't I
come as your sidekick or something. I ought to get
something out of all this.'

'I'll send you a postcard, Sean,' Gordon said and
grinned.

He waylaid Mr Benn at lunch time.

He was delighted.

'Do you know what my name means, Sir?' Gordon
said enthusiastically.

'No idea,' Mr Benn said.

'It means bold,' Gordon said. 'Gordon-the-bold!'

It was the first time he'd told anybody outside the family. And the first time it had ever pleased him.

'And it's very appropriate, then,' Mr Benn said. 'You stuck to your guns and got there in the end. If that isn't bold, what is?'

'With a bit of help from my friends, Sir,' Gordon said. 'It all started with the acting. Acting Brad really helped. Sort of got me going. Made me realise what I could do.'

Mr Benn nodded.

'Since then, when I've not known what to do – what to say – how to go on – I've thought about Brad a lot,' Gordon said. 'I'm very grateful to Brad. And you, Sir. For giving me the chance to act him.'

Chapter Sixteen

Mum was still worried about him going to Canada, of course. She couldn't change that much could she?

But she did start to talk openly about his dad.

'He was a good dad to Amy,' she said to him one time.

It was brilliant hearing something nice for a change.

Another time she said, 'The split was nothing to do with you kids, Gordon. You weren't even born.'

It made up for all those times he'd thought it was his fault.

Then she said, 'It was the two of us, Gordon. Well actually, it was *her*,' she added bitterly. 'If he hadn't met her it might've come all right. Who knows?'

And when he was packing for Canada, she said, 'I wonder what he's like now?'

'I wish you could find someone nice like Eddie or Mr Benn, Mum,' Gordon said shyly. He'd never have dared say that to her before.

'Well who knows...' she said, and smiled at him! 'In a funny way all this has made me feel ready to move on at last. And you're the one I have to thank for that.'

So suddenly the impossible seemed possible, Gordon thought. And if she did meet someone else he'd be happy for her.

Even Amy seemed less moody these days. Though at times he caught her looking at him with a strange look in her eyes.

On the morning of the flight, Mum was in a bit of a state. Eddie was driving them to the airport and all the Wilkinson family were coming to see him off. Gran was coming too, so Sean cadged a lift with her.

At the thought of getting on that plane on his own, Gordon was excited, thrilled, and worked up at the same time. But in the end all he wanted to do was meet his dad – whatever the outcome...

Eddie arrived at the house in the people carrier with Ellie and the kids. Then Sean arrived with Gran.

Eddie saw the cases in the porch and picked them up. 'All this for one!' he said. Amazed.

Amy looked sheepish. 'Well, it's not just for one, actually,' she said.

For a moment what she'd said didn't register with Gordon. It was Eddie who asked how many were going then?

'There's two of us,' Amy said and looked at Gordon, that strange look on her face again.

It was as much a surprise to him as Mum's turnabout. Gordon was in shock.

'It's all right if I come with you, isn't it?' Amy asked him nervously.

Like she needed to ask his permission. Like he was the oldest!

'There's two tickets. Dad always wanted you to come too,' he said. Trying not to admit that part of him was a bit disappointed. He'd got this far on his own. It would have been quite nice to see it through on his own. But then he saw Amy's anxious face and realised how difficult it must have been for her to change her mind. And how badly she must actually want to come. 'It's cool, sis,' he said warmly.

Mum hugged them both.

'When was this decided?' Gran asked.

'I've been thinking about it for days,' Amy said.

'But she only finally made up her mind this morning!' Mum said.

No wonder Mum'd been so frantic all morning, Gordon thought.

'Well I'm delighted,' Gran said.

At the airport, the group hovered round the
boarding gate.

Once past here, Gordon and Amy were on their own.

A steward came up to them. 'Are these the two
young travellers?' he asked. 'Got everything?'

Gran hugged them. Then Mum clutched them to her.

Amy didn't want to let go of Mum. She suddenly
looked like a timid little girl. And, again, it felt like
Gordon was the oldest and the strongest.

He grabbed Amy and shepherded her through.

Then turned back.

One wave only.

'Dad. Here we come,' he said quietly.

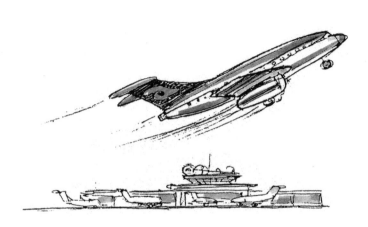